This book belongs to

Quarto is the authority on a wide range of topics.

Quarto educates, entertains and enriches the lives of our readers—enthusiasts and lovers of hands-on living.

www.quartoknows.com

© 2018 Quarto Publishing plc

First published in 2018 by QED Publishing, an imprint of The Quarto Group. The Old Brewery, 6 Blundell Street, London N7 9BH, United Kingdom. T (0)20 7700 6700 F (0)20 7700 8066 www.QuartoKnows.com

A catalogue record for this book is available from the British Library.

ISBN 978-1-78493-920-5

Based on the original story by Virginie Zurcher and Daniel Howarth
Author of adapted text: Katie Woolley
Series Editor: Joyce Bentley
Series Designer: Sarah Peden

Manufactured in Dongguan, China TL102017

9 8 7 6 5 4 3 2 1

MIX
Paper from responsible sources
FSC® C104723

Reading
Gems

The Star
and the Zoo

QED

Little Star was high
up in the sky.

Little Star fell down, down, down.

Bump!

Little Star was sad.

All the animals wanted to help.

But Lion could not get Little Star
back in the sky.

I have a plan.

But Monkey's plan did not work.

But Giraffe could not get Little Star
back in the sky.

Little Star was sad.

Ant wanted to help.

Ant's plan did work.

All the ants could help.

Little Star was high up in the sky.

Story Words

ant

bump

fell

giraffe

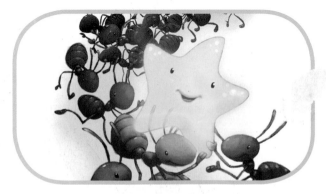

help

lion

monkey

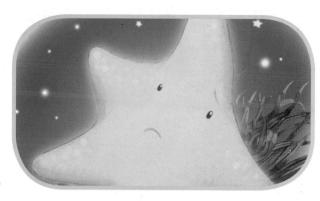

sad

sky

star

zoo

Let's Talk About
The Star and the Zoo

**Look carefully at
the book cover.**

Can you see a star?

What time of day do you
think it is in the story?

What other animals
can you see at the zoo?

**Have a look at the ants
in the picture on page 20.**

How did they get Little Star
back into the sky?

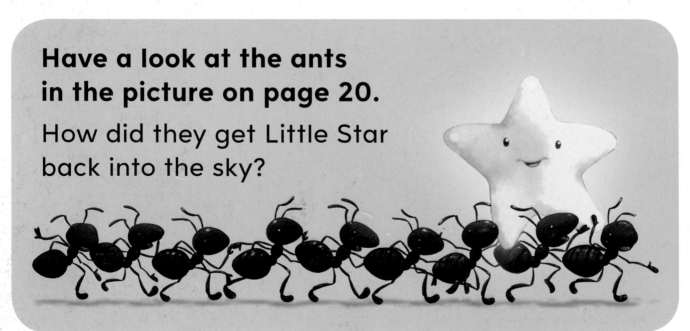

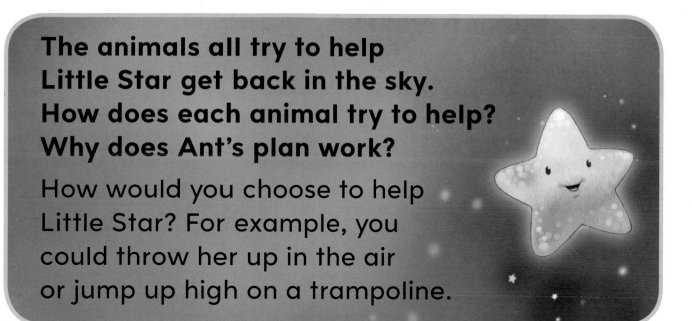

The animals all try to help Little Star get back in the sky. How does each animal try to help? Why does Ant's plan work?

How would you choose to help Little Star? For example, you could throw her up in the air or jump up high on a trampoline.

Look at the zoo on pages 4–5 and pages 8–9.

What different noises might Little Star hear at the zoo in the two pictures?

What noises do you hear at night?

Talk about the end of the story.

Did you like it?

Do you think the star is happy or sad now?

Fun and Games

Look at these pictures and
find the matching words.

star   monkey   giraffe   ant   lion

Look at these pictures of the characters in this story and their feelings. One picture is different. Which one is it?

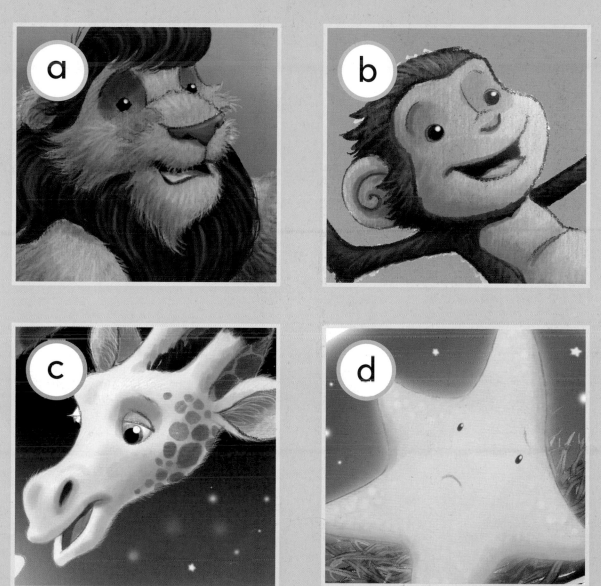

Answer: Picture d is different. The animals are all happy. Little Star is sad.

29

Your Turn

Now that you have read the story,
have a go at telling it in your own words.
Use the pictures below to help you.

GET TO KNOW READING GEMS

Reading Gems is a series of books that has been written for children who are learning to read. The books have been created in consultation with a literacy specialist.

The books fit into four levels, with each level getting more challenging as a child's confidence and reading ability grows. The simple text and fun illustrations provide gradual, structured practice of reading. Most importantly, these books are good stories that are fun to read!

Level 1 is for children who are taking their first steps into reading. Story themes and subjects are familiar to young children, and there is lots of repetition to build reading confidence.

Level 2 is for children who have taken their first reading steps and are becoming readers. Story themes are still familiar but sentences are a bit longer, as children begin to tackle more challenging vocabulary.

Level 3 is for children who are developing as readers. Stories and subjects are varied, and more descriptive words are introduced.

Level 4 is for readers who are rapidly growing in reading confidence and independence. There is less repetition on the page, broader themes are explored and plot lines straddle multiple pages.

The Star and the Zoo is all about learning to work together. It explores themes of kindness, friendship and teamwork.

Level 1

Little Star was sad.

Ant wanted to help.

I have a plan.

Short sentences ✓

Simple vocabulary ✓

Lots of repetition ✓

Pictures and words support one another ✓